HARRY
IS BORED

Harry strutted into the TV room. "I'm bored," said Harry.

I was sitting at the card table, doing a jigsaw puzzle. I didn't turn round. "Don't start," I warned him.

Harry padded across the floor and stopped by my chair. Then he turned his back on me. "Really bored." His tail thudded against the carpet.

Harry is a cat. He's a big, fat, grey cat. Except, of course, that he's not really a cat. He's really an alien from the planet Arcana. The extraterrestrials from Arcana always take on the form of cats when they travel in our solar system. Harry had been visiting the Earth for ages, but this was the first time he'd ever visited the twentieth century. It was also the first time that his spaceship had ever disappeared and left him behind. I met Harry one rainy day by the dustbins at the end of our road. I wasn't half surprised the first time he started talking to me, I can tell you that. My name is Sara Jane, but my family call me Chicken because I had this stuffed chicken I dragged around with me when I was little. I can't break them of the habit.

CONTENTS

HARRY
THE
EXPLORER

Dyan Sheldon

Illustrations by
Sue Heap

WALKER BOOKS
AND SUBSIDIARIES
LONDON · BOSTON · SYDNEY

For
Minnie

First published 1991 by Walker Books Ltd
87 Vauxhall Walk, London SE11 5HJ

This edition published 1997

2 4 6 8 10 9 7 5 3

Text © 1991 Dyan Sheldon
Illustrations © 1991 Sue Heap
Cover illustration © 1997 Sue Heap

Printed in Great Britain

British Library Cataloguing in Publication Data
A catalogue record for this book is
available from the British Library.

ISBN 0-7445-5291-5

J109, 646
£3.99

For Harry and Chicken read "hilarity and chaos" in this second madcap story about a girl and her troublesome extraterrestrial cat!

Dyan Sheldon is a children's writer, adult novelist, humourist and cat-lover. Her children's titles include *The Whales' Song* and, for Walker Books, *Sky Watching*, *A Night to Remember*, *Elena the Frog*, and three stories about an alien cat and his human minder, Harry and Chicken.

Sue Heap has illustrated a number of children's books, including all three Harry and Chicken stories, *Elena the Frog*, *Tillie McGillie's Fantastical Chair*, and the picture books *Mouse Party*, *Little Chicken Chicken* and *Town Parrot*.

"Harry," I said sternly, "you know what my parents said. No trouble." They'd said that because from the first moment I'd brought Harry home with me he'd been nothing but trouble.

"I knew London was supposed to be damp," said Harry, "but this is ridiculous." He sighed. "It's been raining for five days," he informed me.

"You're not exactly a prisoner. And besides, you don't do much except eat and sleep anyway."

Harry jumped on to the desk, stretching out. Bits of the jigsaw fell to the floor.

"There's not much I can do when it's always raining, is there?" he snapped. "Here I am, a visitor from another planet, and all I've learned about life in the twentieth century is that shopping centres are dangerous and that you need an umbrella."

Harry's mention of shopping centres was a reference to his one disastrous trip out of our neighbourhood, to the Millwood Shopping Centre. Harry claimed that several hundred people had chased him down the length of Level 2. My mother said it was more like ten.

"That was your own fault," I pointed out.

"It was not my own fault," said Harry huffily. "Those people were violent, Chicken. They reminded me of the barbarians who sacked Rome." Harry has hundreds of stories about his visits to Earth. Nothing has ever happened here without Harry's help.

"Harry, please, you're exaggerating." Harry always exaggerates.

"Here I am," he sighed, "a being with a superior intelligence, and the most exciting thing I do all day is guess what's for pudding."

"Well," I suggested, "since you've got such a superior intelligence, why don't you help me with my puzzle instead of lying all over it?"

Harry rolled over on to his side. "What is it?"

"It's a picture of a rowing boat on a lake."

"A picture of a rowing boat on a lake?" Harry yawned. "That's what you've been doing for the past three days?"

"Yes," I said, "it is. I've finished all my schoolwork. And I've read all my books. And you won't play any of my games with me..."

He rolled over on to his other side. "Here you are on this terrific planet, with all sorts of adventures to be had, and you sit in a room putting together a picture of a rowing boat on a lake."

I didn't like his tone of voice. "Harry..." I began.

"I don't understand you, Chicken," said Harry. "Why don't you ever want to go out? Make some new friends? Have some fun?"

My mother would have been surprised if she'd known how much like her Harry could sound. There was no use trying to explain to either of them that since my best friend Kim moved away there was nowhere to go and no one to meet. "Harry..." I began again.

"I bet you've never even wondered what's on the other side of that lake," said Harry dreamily.

"Harry, I —"

Harry got up and sat right by the window with his nose on the glass. "Have you, Chicken? Have you even once wondered what's on the other side of that lake?"

"Harry," I said, "it's just a picture." I looked down. Of course it was just a picture.

Harry's ears bent back. My mother called it Harry's one trick, bending his ears back. "Isn't that sweet?" she said. "I've never seen a cat do that before." But I was beginning to realize it had a sinister meaning all of its own.

"Just a picture?" he purred. "Look out of the window, Chicken. What do you see?"

He'd bent his ears back the first time I tried to give him cat food. (It ended up all over me and the ceiling.) He'd bent his ears back the last time Bella the beagle came into our garden. (She ended up caught in the sprinkler.) He'd bent his ears back when the vet tried to give him his injection. (The vet said he didn't usually ban animals from his surgery, but in Harry's case he was making an exception.)

When Harry bent his ears back it meant he was going to cause trouble.

"I'm not doing it."

"Not doing what?" asked Harry, all innocent. He swivelled his head round. It made him look like an owl. "All I asked was what you saw out of the window."

"I know what's out of the window," I said, staring right into those big round eyes.

"There's a couple of trees."

Harry smiled. "What else?"

"My mother's garden."

He nodded.

"And the fence that goes round the garden. And the bird table. And the lawn. And the gnomes my grandmother gave us for Christmas."

"And the rain," said Harry. "Don't forget the rain."

"Of course," I said, wondering if I could relax now. "And the rain."

Harry smiled again. It wasn't really a comforting sight. "So," he said, "why won't you look out of the window?"

"I … well…" Sometimes you just know you shouldn't do something. Like you know you shouldn't borrow your brother's binoculars because you're going to lose them. Or you know you shouldn't play your sister's favourite record because you're going to scratch it. Or you know for absolute certain that if you try to get the sweet jar down from the top shelf it's going to break. But you do it anyway. This time I knew I shouldn't look out of the window. The problem was, I didn't really know why.

Harry's ears twitched.

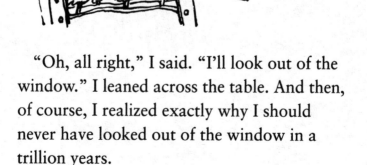

"Oh, all right," I said. "I'll look out of the window." I leaned across the table. And then, of course, I realized exactly why I should never have looked out of the window in a trillion years.

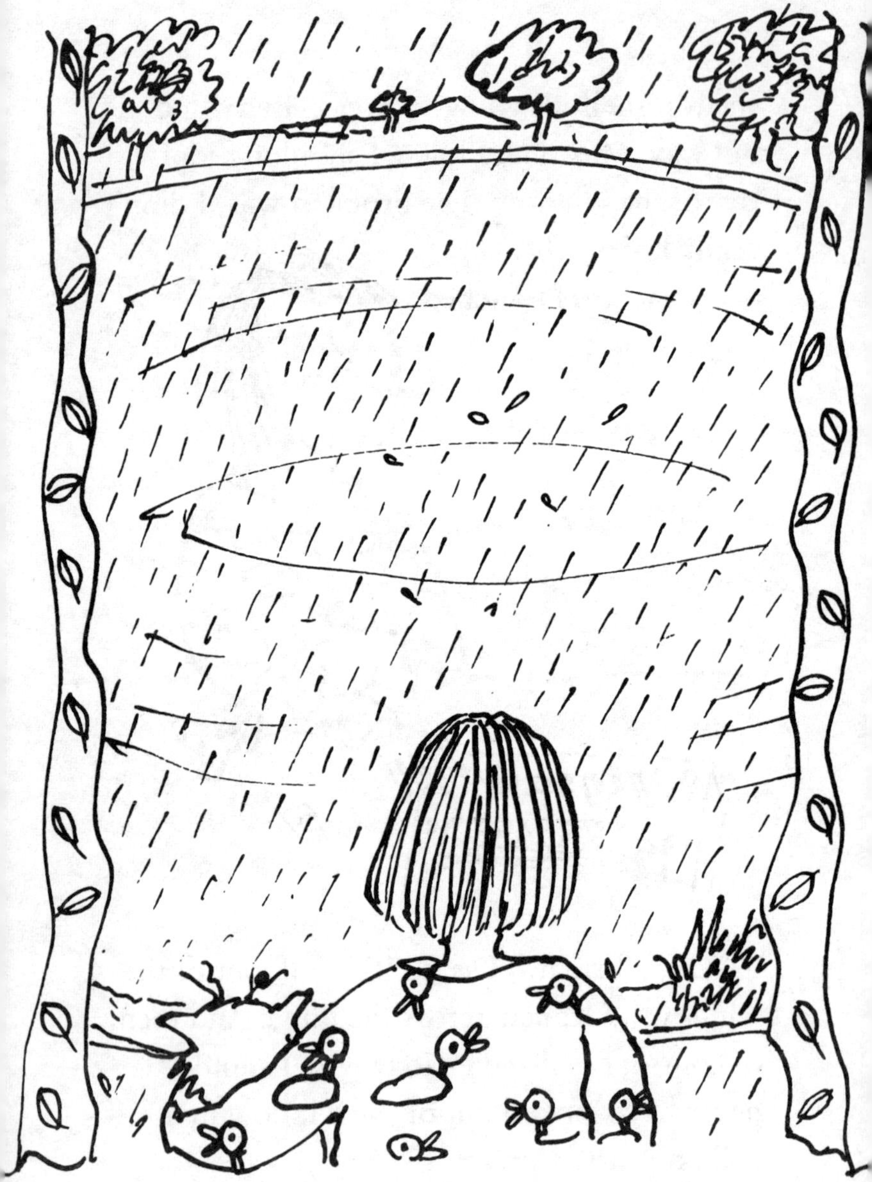

There right in front of us, where my mother's garden and the trees and the grass and the fence and the bird table and the garden gnomes usually were, was the lake that should have been in the puzzle. But I wasn't really surprised. I was getting used to the fact that when you live with a creature from a distant galaxy, time and space can do funny things.

"Well?" asked Harry. "Shall we go and see what's on the other side?"

"Oh, Harry," I said, "I don't think this is a very good idea."

Harry flicked his tail. "Oh, pooh pooh," said Harry.

GETTING OUT
OF THE DOOR

As quietly as we could, Harry and I tiptoed into the hall. After all, there was no good reason for disturbing my mother. My mother's a very busy woman. She's a potter. She's a potter who hates being disturbed for no good reason when she's busy throwing a teapot or painting a plate. I put on my anorak and my wellies. It never rains on the planet Arcana so Harry, of course, had no rain gear. I put him under my anorak. We crept towards the back door.

We were half-way across the kitchen when a sound behind us made me jump.

"Just a minute!" said my mother in her

no-nonsense mother voice. "Where do you two think you're going?"

"Us?" I asked, turning to face her. The sound I'd heard must have been the kettle banging on the counter. I'd been sure my mother was in her workroom, working, but instead she was sneaking around the kitchen, making herself some blackberry tea.

"Yes, you." She had clay in her hair and a suspicious look on her face.

"We're going for a walk," I said. I tried to sound surprised that she would even ask me such a question.

My mother looked out of the window, checking. The sun wasn't shining. The birds weren't singing. It was what my father always called a good day for fish. "In this weather?"

"Yes," I said. "We need some exercise." My mother is very in favour of exercise.

"*We?*" She pointed to Harry, peeking out from my jacket. "It doesn't look as if that cat is planning to do much walking."

"He doesn't like to get his feet wet," I explained. "You know how sensitive he is."

"Um," said my mother, frowning at Harry. She'd forgiven him for his behaviour at the shopping centre, but she still hadn't forgiven him for biting the vet. "I'm surprised he's not taking a bag of food with him."

Harry's ears perked up at this. Harry has a reputation for eating a lot. It's a reputation he's earned. I ignored him. "We're not going far," I assured her. I hoped this was true. "We just need a little air. You know," I smiled, "we've been cooped up in the house for *days*." My mother hates any child of hers to be cooped up in the house for days. She's always trying to shove you out of the door. Go to the park. Go for a bike ride. Go out on your skateboard. And ever since my best friend Kim moved away she's had a new cry. Go and make some new friends. As if all you have to do is stroll down the street and all these people are going to come rushing up to you, begging to be your friend.

"Well…" She still didn't look too sure. "As long as you don't go too far."

"We won't, Mum." I kissed the top of Harry's head. "Will we, Harry?" Harry purred. "You see," I said, "we promise."

She was still looking suspicious. "Chicken," she said, "just out of curiosity…"

I smiled helpfully. There's nothing worse than a curious mother. "Yes?"

"If you and Harry are going for a walk, why don't you go out the front way?"

J109,646

"What?"

"Why don't you go out the front?" she repeated. "Or are you just going to walk round the garden?"

"No, no," I said. "No, we're not going to just walk round the garden. Only we're here, in the kitchen, aren't we? And here's the back door..." I put my hand on the doorknob.

"Well," she said, her Sherlock Holmes expression still on her face, "I suppose that as long as you're going out you can make yourself useful."

Harry sighed. He isn't big on being useful.

"Of course, Mum, what is it?"

She handed me some change. "Stop at the shop and get me a pint of milk, a loaf of bread, and a pound of tomatoes."

"One pint of milk, one loaf of bread and one pound of tomatoes coming up," I said cheerily.

"And Chicken," said my mother as I opened the door, "mind the puddles, won't you? And don't get too wet."

I pulled up my hood. "You can count on me, Mum," I said. And then I shut the door behind us and stepped into the yard.

HARRY
THE SAILOR

I stood on the garden path and looked back at the house. My mother was at the window watching us. From the expression on her face I could tell that what she saw through the window were her tulips and her daffodils and her rose bushes, bending in the rain. She saw the bird table, which was now more like a bird bath. She saw the two grinning gnomes: one riding his snail and the other one with the rake in his hand. She saw me and Harry, standing in the downpour, getting soaking wet.

She knocked on the glass. "Sara Jane!" she shouted. "Sara Jane! Don't you want an umbrella?"

"No thanks, Mum," I shouted back. "No thanks, we're fine. Really." After all, you can't row a boat with an umbrella in your hand, can you?

Because what I saw in front of us was a lake. It was greeny-blue, just like in the picture on the box. And the green rowing boat was tied up by the shore, just like in the picture on the box. There was only one thing that was different.

"I don't understand," I said to Harry, as I untied the boat. I was relieved to see that there weren't any pieces missing from it. "Why is it still raining? It's not raining in the puzzle."

"Chicken," sighed Harry, peering up at me from inside my anorak. All I could see of him were his eyes, like moons, and the tip of his nose. "What do I look like to you? A weatherman? A magician?"

"No, Harry," I said, climbing in. "You look like a cat."

"Then why do you ask me stupid

questions?" asked Harry. "It's raining because it's raining."

I sat down on the worn wooden seat. I picked up the oars. "Now what?" I asked.

Harry sighed again. He has absolutely no patience. "Now you row." Harry's head popped up under my chin, looking out across the water. "So," he said, "what do you think's at the other side of this lake?"

I squinted through the rain. It was hard to see anything. "Well, I don't know," I said. "I really haven't thought about it." We started gliding across the water.

"Well think about it now," said Harry.

The oars were heavy. "Well, I suppose there could be a dock or something like that on the other side," I huffed.

"Um," said Harry.

"Or another boat," I puffed.

"Um," said Harry.

"Or maybe a duck or two."

Harry's head was nodding. "You certainly don't have an overactive imagination, do you,

Chicken?" he asked sleepily. "Where would we be if Columbus had had an imagination like yours?"

We'd probably be right where we were, I thought to myself. Besides, I didn't see what imagination had to do with anything. Columbus didn't discover America because of his great imagination. He discovered it because he got lost.

"What's that supposed to mean?" I panted. Rowing in the rain is not an easy thing to do. Especially not with a fat cat on your lap.

"It means that there might be anything at all on the other side of this lake. A tropical rain forest. A family of bathing rhinoceroses.

An encampment of Tibetan horsemen." His tail tickled my nose. "But all you can imagine are ducks."

"I think this lake is meant to be in England," I said. "We don't really go in for tropical rain forests or Tibetan horsemen or things like that in this country."

"Those were just examples," said Harry. He could sound really snotty when he wanted to. "The point is that the lake in the puzzle is just a picture. There isn't anything on the other side. I was trying to encourage you to think of what you'd *like* to find there."

"Right now what I'd like to find," I gasped, "is an outboard motor. This rowing is hard

work." I pulled in the oars and looked around. I'd been so busy that I hadn't noticed it was getting windy. Thunder rumbled through the sky. The lake was choppy. The boat was starting to rock back and forth.

"Wow, look at this, Harry! This really is an adventure!" For the first time I was feeling excited. This was the sort of thing Kim would have loved. She would have said it was a gas. That's what Kim always called something she really liked, "a real gas".

"Chicken," said Harry.

"Think of it! We're out on a lake in the middle of a storm! We're crossing into unknown territory. Anything could happen." Wait till I wrote to Kim.

"Chicken," said Harry.

For the first time I noticed that his voice sounded funny. I looked down. He was sort of slumped against me. "Harry, what's wrong?"

"Chicken," he said, "Chicken, you'll have to pull over."

"Pull over? What are you talking about? I can't pull over. We're in the middle of the lake."

"I don't feel well, Chicken," said Harry. He certainly didn't look well. "I'm not used to being in a boat."

"Wait a minute," I said. "I thought you sailed the Atlantic with Columbus."

"That," said Harry, burping, "was a long, long time ago."

THE OTHER SIDE OF THE LAKE

Harry complained the rest of the way. Harry is never too tired, or too wet, or too cold, or too unwell to complain. Chicken, can't you go a little slower? Chicken, can't you go a little faster? Chicken, do you have to make the boat bob up and down so much?

"This is nothing like sailing with Columbus," moaned Harry. "Sailing with Columbus was fun. His sailors were always singing."

"Singing?" I grunted. "You expect me to row this boat in the pouring rain and sing at the same time?"

But Harry was busy sticking his head under

my armpit. "Columbus' ships were warm and dry," came the muffled reply.

"His ships were warm and dry?" I laughed. "In 1492?"

A pink nose appeared at the neck of my anorak. "Well, pretty warm and dry," said Harry. "At least you could go down below." His whiskers twitched. "The only thing below us is fish." Harry hates fish. "At least you didn't have to duck the oars the whole time," grumbled Harry. "At least there was food."

"I thought you didn't feel well," I pointed out. "How can you think about food if you don't feel well?"

Burp, burp, burp, groan. "I'm planning for when I feel better," said Harry.

I rowed and rowed. I tried to ignore Harry. I tried to imagine that I was a great explorer, sailing into the unknown. I tried to imagine myself with Columbus.

I was on the *Niña*. Or maybe it was the *Pinta* or the *Santa Maria*. Anyway, I was on this ship. The deck was packed with singing

sailors. Singing sailors and one fat grey cat.
The days passed slowly. The weeks went by
without any sight of land. We were running

low on food and water. I stared out across the ocean, wondering if we were going to fall off the edge of the Earth or not. Some of the sailors stopped singing. They wanted to mutiny. The cat talked to them. He told them that they were on this wonderful planet where there were all sorts of adventures to be had. "Who knows what's across this ocean?" said the cat. "Tropical rain forests. Tibetan horsemen. Rhinoceroses. You don't want to sit in your rooms in dirty old Europe when you could be having all these great adventures, do you?" he asked them. The sailors looked at each other. "Well," they said, "when you put it like that…" We sailed on and on. And then one day, there in the distance, I spied a tiny dot on the horizon. Was it a whale? Was it a mirage? Was it a sea monster? Was it…?

I looked over my shoulder. Yes, there was something straight ahead of us. "Harry!" I cried. "Harry, look! Land ahoy!" Although, to tell the truth, I wasn't absolutely positive that it was land. The storm made it difficult to see, and we were still so far away. It might turn out to be an iceberg. Or dolphins. Or a ship. I caught my breath. It might be a pirate ship. Now that would be exciting.

Harry's head reappeared. "Oh, really, Chicken," he said shortly. "Do you have to be so melodramatic?"

"I'm not being melodramatic," I said, a little hurt. I thought he wanted me to get into the spirit of things. "There's definitely something there."

Harry leaned forward. "Where?"

"There," I said, pointing. "Right there."

Harry's stomach growled. He was feeling better. "I don't recognize it," said Harry. He made it sound as if anything he couldn't recognize couldn't be too interesting. "What do you think it is?"

"Well," I grunted, rowing hard. "I'm not really sure."

We were just getting close enough to make out what it wasn't. It wasn't a tropical rain forest. It wasn't an encampment of Tibetan horsemen. It wasn't a family of squeaky-clean rhinoceroses. I couldn't help feeling a little disappointed. It certainly wasn't a pirate ship.

"Are those buildings?" asked Harry, his ears twitching. He seemed to be perking up.

"Yes!" I cried. I could make out a high wall. I could see the rooftops and towers rising behind it. It was like one of those magical kingdoms you read about in storybooks. Magical kingdoms, I knew, always appear suddenly. One minute they're not there; and the next minute they're materializing out of the mist. Or, in this case, materializing out of the steady downpour. But one thing is always true: you can only see them if you really believe. "Wow," I said. "Maybe we've discovered a lost city or something like that." I wondered if there would be princesses and princes; if there would be magicians and genii and two-headed monsters; if there would be pirates, taking a break from the sea.

"I don't care whether it's lost or not," sniffed Harry. "I just hope it has a decent snack bar. Adventure always gives me an appetite."

Sleeping gives Harry an appetite.

I left him under the seat while I pulled the boat to shore.

"So now what do we do?" I called over my shoulder. I tied the rope to a tree. "Do you think we can find a way through the wall? A secret entrance or something?" I went back for my seasick extraterrestrial. "Do you think we can, Harry? Do you think we can get into the secret city?" The only reply was the sound of the rain. "Harry?" I looked under the seat where I'd left him. No Harry. I looked under the other two seats. No Harry. No Harry up the tree. No Harry in the lake. No Harry on the wall. But I wasn't surprised. I was getting used to the fact that Harry was never where you expected him to be, when you expected him to be there. "Harry!" I called. "Harry, where are you?"

I turned back to the wall. It was very smooth and very high. There was no way Harry could have got over it. At least I didn't think there was. "Harry!" I screamed. "Harry! Fun's fun, but you've got to come out now." If he wasn't on the other side, where was he? I looked around. No ladders. No doors. No fat grey cat. But there was an enormous, gnarled old tree a few yards from the wall. I decided to climb it, to get a better view. I climbed slowly. The branches were dense and slippery. I climbed very slowly. At last, panting, I came to a rest.

There before me was my magical kingdom. It was beautiful. The buildings were large and their windows seemed to sparkle in the rain. All the houses on the street where I live are white, but these were all painted in different colours – pinks and greens and blues and yellows. There were large, saucer-like discs and strange shapes twisted out of metal attached to the rooftops. In one garden there was a pool filled with gigantic goldfish.

In another there were about a hundred tiny wooden planes spinning around on poles. I'd never seen anything like it before. Where was I? What sort of people lived here?

"Harry!" I shouted. I remembered something else about magic kingdoms. The wizards and elves and monsters who live in them don't always like visitors. "Harry, you'd better come out. Now!"

HARRY
THE
EXPLORER

So there I was, sitting in this tree in what for
all I knew was a major hurricane, looking
down on this strange place where anything
might happen. Part of me felt sort of excited.
And part of me felt scared. But most of me
was feeling cold and wet. And angry. If Harry
really wanted to have an adventure with me,
why had he abandoned me the minute we
landed? What sort of a friend was that? If he
really cared about me, why had he dragged
me away from my safe, warm home and left
me all alone in a tree? I huddled in my
anorak. All my best friends were leaving me
alone lately.

I looked up and down the row of buildings, but there was nothing that even looked a little like a cat. I sneezed. That's it, I thought, I've had enough of this. He'll just have to find his own way back. I'm going home. I rowed over here by myself, and I can row back. I turned round to climb down. The only thing behind me was the lake. I couldn't see our house or any of the other houses in our street. I couldn't see our fence or the garden shed of the people next door. The lake looked a lot bigger than it had before. "So what?" I said to myself. "Of course you can't see the other side. What are you worried about? You crossed it once, you can cross it again." I stared down at the lake. And then it struck me. The lake was all I could see. The boat was gone. This was crazy.

"Harry!" I screamed. "Harry, where are you?" Harry couldn't have taken the boat – he hates any sort of physical exercise. So if Harry hadn't taken it, who had? An evil knight? A troll? A pirate?

I could hear barking a few buildings down the row. Don't be silly, I told myself. Just because you hear a dog barking doesn't mean it has anything to do with Harry.

"Harry, I'm serious!" I shouted. "If you don't come out right this minute I'm leaving you here by yourself! You'll miss tea!"

The barking grew louder.

On the other hand, it might have something to do with Harry. It was worth a look, wasn't it? A sudden frightening thought occurred to me. A thought more frightening than the thought of what I might find on the other side of the wall. If I didn't find Harry I might never get back home. I turned to look across the lake again. It seemed to go on for ever. "Be brave," I told myself. "Think of Christopher Columbus." But instead I thought of Harry. When I got my hands on him I was going to wring his neck. I lowered myself on to the wall. I jumped to the ground. The barking grew even louder. Without a second thought, I hurled myself over the fence and into the nearest garden.

Isn't it funny how things change when you get closer to them? Because, now that I was down on the ground, this new land didn't look quite the same. It was still beautiful. It was still strange. There might still be pirates behind the doors or princesses locked in towers. But seeing my secret kingdom from a distance had been like looking at a picture. Now that I was running in it, it was real. These were real houses. They had curtains and plants at the windows. Some of them needed painting. Someone lived in these houses. These were real gardens. There was a bike I hadn't noticed before on its side in the grass. Kids played here. I heaved myself over the second fence. There were chairs and a table and a bird table. Families sat outside on summer evenings. People mowed the grass and dug up the weeds. They watered the flowers. They fed the birds.

I heaved myself over the third fence. The barking was getting closer. "Harry!" I was really shouting now. I had to shout, to be heard above the noise of this lunatic dog. But I was also shouting because another awful thought had occurred to me. What if I couldn't find Harry because he wasn't here? What if his spaceship had suddenly returned for him and he'd gone back to Arcana? He'd said that was the way it would happen. It would just reappear the way it had disappeared. Snap. Then what was I going to do? I might have to spend the rest of my life in this place. In someone else's garden.

It wouldn't bother my brother and sister. They'd be able to use my room. They wouldn't have to share anything with me any more. They'd never have to mind me when my parents went out. There would always be enough ice-cream to go round. And it wasn't really going to bother Kim, was it? She was in Manchester, going to a new school, making new friends. But my parents were going to be really upset. They liked me. And besides, who would help my dad wash the car if I never got back home? Who was going to help my mother pack up the things she made for the shops?

"Harry!" I yelled. "Harry, I'm counting to three. One!" I scrambled over the next wall, and landed in a bed of flowers. The barking was coming from inside the house. "Two!" I was afraid to move in case I trampled on something else. "Three!"

I looked up, my eyes on the back door. Something was happening. All of a sudden a grey streak flew out of the door. Right behind it was a killer Jack Russell. The grey streak

leapt over the fence and into the next garden.
I thought of Superman, able to leap tall
buildings in a single bound. The Jack Russell
went right after it.

"Harry!" I screamed. "Harry! I'm here!"

The grey streak cleared the next fence
without a pause. The Jack Russell was right
behind it. I'd never seen Harry move like that
before. Not even in the shopping centre. He
was really impressive. He could have been in
the Olympics. I wished my family could see
him now. My mother was always going on

about how lazy Harry was. My sister called him Hoover because of the way he ate. My brother made jokes about his size. Even my father seemed to find him amusing. "Why don't you do a little intergalactic travelling, Harry?" my father would say, lifting him out of his chair so he could sit down. But this would make them change their minds. Unless, of course, the Jack Russell ate Harry. Then it wouldn't matter what they thought.

I jumped out of the flower bed, stomping on a few hundred innocent plants as I went. "Don't worry, Harry!" I yelled. "I'll save you!" I sort of thought I heard a door open and someone shout as I flung myself over the fence. But I couldn't stop now.

HARRY HOUDINI

It was in the garden with the conservatory attached to the back of the house and the goldfish in the pond that the Jack Russell and I lost Harry. Harry's very fond of tuna fish sandwiches and he has nothing against a plate of cod and chips (unless it's got vinegar on it), but he can't stand real fish. I think something awful must have happened when he sailed with Columbus.

Harry landed in the pond. I was just in time to see him disappear in a spray of water and lily pads. There was a squeal of terror. And then there was nothing. No sound. No splashing. No cat. Either he went up on the roof and through one of the windows on the first floor, or he went up on the roof and vanished into thin air. But the windows were all shut tight. Maybe Harry was a magician after all. One minute he was there and the next he wasn't. The Jack Russell was beside me, jumping straight up and down in the air, barking his head off. I was standing next to

him gazing at the spot where I'd last seen that flash of grey. For a second I thought there was a face at one of the windows, but when I looked again it was gone.

"Oh, shut up, will you?" I said to the dog. "You're going to have the whole neighbourhood out after us."

Talk about being able to predict the future. No sooner were the words out of my mouth than the conservatory door flew open and a woman marched into the garden. Except that she had a newspaper over her head and a spoon in her hand she looked pretty normal. She definitely wasn't a princess or a pirate, although the way she was swinging the spoon about she might have been a witch. A very upset witch.

"What's all this noise?" she screamed at me. "What are you trying to do? Wake the dead?" Her eyes fell on the Jack Russell, dementedly jumping up and down as though he'd swallowed a spring or something. "Is that your dog?"

I looked at the Jack Russell.

"Is it?" she screamed more loudly. "Is that your dog?"

I opened my mouth to answer.

"No," panted a voice to my left. "That's *my* dog."

The woman and I both turned. Heaving himself over the fence was a very wet man. His face was red and he didn't have any shoes on, just socks. I felt like I sort of knew him. A vague memory of seeing him in the video shop with a small boy floated through my mind. But that, of course, was impossible.

They don't have video shops in magic kingdoms, do they?

"Suzie Q!" shouted the man, still out of breath. "Suzie Q, heel!"

Suzie Q? The killer Jack Russell was called Suzie Q? I looked over at her. She landed on the ground like a rock.

And then, for no reason, instead of yelling at Suzie Q for causing such a commotion, the man turned on me. "And as for you!" he roared. "Is that your cat?"

I was beginning to feel a little like Dorothy in *The Wizard of Oz*.

The woman in the doorway looked round. "What cat?" she asked. Newsprint was beginning to run down her arms. "What are you talking about? I don't see any cat."

"Cat?" I repeated.

"Don't play the innocent with me," shouted the man. "You know what cat I mean. I saw you in my garden." He pointed at me but looked at the woman. "This child's cat," he said, "got into my house."

I tried to look suitably shocked. The woman just stared at him.

"This child's cat," he said, shaking his finger, "ate Suzie Q's food."

The woman and I both looked over at Suzie Q. Her tail was wagging away, squelching in the mud. You could tell she was just waiting to start barking and jumping up and down again. I thought I saw a smile flicker on the woman's face, but it was hard to tell because the rain was making everything blurry.

The man hadn't finished. "This child's cat," he said, now shaking his fist at me, "opened my fridge and helped itself to a piece of roast beef."

This time I was sure I saw the woman fighting back a smile.

"There's no telling what it would have eaten if Suzie Q hadn't stopped it," he spluttered.

"Don't be ridiculous," said the woman. "Cats can't open fridges."

"Are you calling me a liar?"

"No, of course not," said the woman. "All I'm saying is…"

But the man interrupted her. "This child's cat upset my dog." He took a step towards me.

"Upset your dog?" I said. I took a step towards him. "Your dog upset my cat. None of this would have happened if it weren't for your dog." I looked accusingly at Suzie Q.

The man looked accusingly at me. "Your cat broke into my house!" he raged.

"Oh, for goodness sake," said the woman. "Cats don't break into people's houses…"

But the man was still looking at me. "This one did," he said. He took another step forward. "And you," he said, "you trampled through my garden."

"And you've trampled through mine," the woman said to him.

The man lunged forward and grabbed hold of my arm. "Where is that cat?" he shouted.

"He's lost," I shouted back. "Your dog lost him." I tried to pull away.

Suzie Q forgot that she was supposed to be heeling and started barking and bouncing again.

"You take your hands off that child!" shouted the woman.

"I'll do no such thing!" screamed the man.
"And when I get my hands on that cat I'm
going to skin it alive!"

The next thing I knew the woman was
standing beside us. She belted the man with
her spoon. If she was a witch she was a
good one.

HARRY'S HIDEOUT

The woman with the spoon was Mrs Andreas. Mrs Andreas invited us into her house so that we could discuss what had happened in a calm and reasonable manner.

"After all," she said to Mr Alvarez, "you and I are adults." He rubbed his head. She apologized for hitting him with the soup spoon.

Mrs Andreas hung up my anorak to dry. She made me take off my wellies and put on a sweater. She made Mr Alvarez take off his socks and put on a pair of her husband's slippers. She gave him a towel to dry himself with and a towel to dry off Suzie Q. She made us all tea. She would have given us biscuits, too, but the biscuits were all gone.

"Now, isn't that funny?" said Mrs Andreas. "I was sure I had a whole tin."

Mrs Andreas poured the tea. "Now then," she said. "What do you say we all shake hands and make friends? After all," she said, "there's no harm done. Milk or lemon?"

"Uh, thank you very much, Mrs Andreas, but I really don't want any tea. I've got to find my cat."

"No harm done?" said Mr Alvarez. "What are you talking about? My garden's a shambles. My dinner's gone. You should see the mess in my kitchen."

"My garden's a shambles, too," said Mrs Andreas, looking right at Mr Alvarez. "Thanks to you. And look at my floor."

We looked at the floor. It was covered in muddy footprints.

"That's beside the point," said Mr Alvarez. He shook his teaspoon at me. "We don't want young hooligans running wild in the streets with their vicious animals."

Mrs Andreas looked over at Suzie Q, sitting on Mr Alvarez's lap with a towel over her, quivering. If he let go of her for a second she was going to start jumping in the air again.

"The only vicious animal I've seen this

afternoon," said Mrs Andreas, "is that dog."
She handed Mr Alvarez his tea. "And anyway,
you certainly can't call Sara Jane here a
hooligan."

Mr Alvarez glared at me as though a
hooligan was just what he could call me.

Mrs Andreas smiled at me kindly. "She's
just a little girl whose cat is lost."

I stared back at them like a little girl whose
cat is lost. "He's my only friend," I said sadly.

And then I really did feel sad when I
realized this was true.

"It's no wonder you have no
friends," snapped Mr Alvarez,
"the way you carry on."

I pushed back my chair.
"Mrs Andreas," I
said, "I've really got
to find Harry."

"You can't go back
out in this," said Mrs
Andreas, pointing
out of the window.

"You don't know Harry," I said. "He's really very sensitive." I glared at Mr Alvarez. "He might drown or something."

Mrs Andreas gave me her best comforting-mother smile. "I'm sure he's found somewhere warm and dry by now," she said.

Mr Alvarez took the sugar bowl from Mrs Andreas. "I moved here because this is a quiet, peaceful neighbourhood," he said. "I didn't move here so that my house could be invaded by ravenous cats."

"Well, if you ask me," said Mrs Andreas, "this neighbourhood is a little too quiet." She smiled at me. "Do you know, we've been here for three months, and this is the first time I've met any of my neighbours?"

Neighbours? A new thought was beginning to occur to me. Didn't a few of the houses behind ours have satellite dishes? I looked out of the window. Didn't that weathervane seem awfully familiar? Hadn't I seen that bench before? And those little planes in that other garden... Wasn't my father always

joking about the man behind us and his windmills?

Mrs Andreas smiled at Mr Alvarez. "I'm enjoying this afternoon," she announced.

"Well I'm not," said Mr Alvarez. He slurped his tea. "Three months?" he said to Mrs Andreas. "We've been here six."

"Is that so?" said Mrs Andreas.

Mr Alvarez nodded. "Six months, one week, and four days."

"Well, that's quite a while," said Mrs Andreas. "You must have a lot of friends by now."

Instead of answering, Mr Alvarez turned to me. "Haven't I seen you in the video shop?" he asked.

Don't waste your time sitting in a room, Chicken. Don't waste your time doing a silly jigsaw puzzle. Get out and see the world. Have an adventure. Some adventure. We hadn't gone anywhere at all. This wasn't a magic kingdom, it was the row of houses behind ours! All we'd done was cross the back garden. That's all we'd done. It was as though Columbus had set off for India and discovered Spain. If we'd wanted to see these houses, we could have stayed at home. You could see the whole row from my brother's room. And we would have been safe and sound. To get into Ben's room you have to squeeze through the door because there's always so much junk piled behind it. And you have to climb over his model railway, which takes up most of the floor. And you can't sit down because there's always stuff on the bed and the budgie cage is on the only chair. And the smell of old socks makes you want to puke. But it doesn't rain in Ben's room. Small, mad dogs don't attack you in Ben's room. No one yells at you but Ben. And if I'd been in Ben's room I would have known where Harry was.

"The video shop?" I said. "Maybe."

"So you come from round here, too," said Mrs Andreas.

I wasn't really sure any more whether I did or not. It really had looked magical. It really had. Like anything might have happened. Like a girl and her cat could really have had an adventure. How could it look so strange and mysterious and be right on the other side of my mother's roses? "Well..." I said.

"Perhaps you know my daughter, Julia. Maybe you go to the same school."

I shook my head. "No," I said, "no, I don't know anyone called..."

"Julia!" called Mrs Andreas. "Julia!" She bounded out of her chair and grabbed hold of me. "Just go straight up," she said, tugging me into the hall.

"Er, Mrs Andreas," I said, "I'm sure your daughter's very nice, but I am pretty worried about my cat, you know. I can't go home without…"

"First door on the left," said Mrs Andreas. She gave me a little shove. "Just go straight up."

I stood there. Mrs Andreas went back into the kitchen and started talking to Mr Alvarez about where he used to live and where she used to live and how hard it was making new friends. What an afternoon I was having. To think, I could have been safe at home finishing my puzzle, and instead I was in some strange house, catless, wearing somebody else's jumper, walking up somebody else's stairs.

I knocked on the first door on the left. "Julia?" I called. "Julia, your mother said…"

"Go away!"

"Julia? Your mother said…"

"Oh, all right, come in!"

I opened the door. Sitting on the bed was a girl I'd seen at school. She was a class behind me.

Next to her, his head on the pillow, a blanket
over him, and biscuit crumbs dribbled down
the front of him, was a big, grey cat.

"He's your cat, isn't he?" said Julia.

"Harry!" I cried.

"You're going to take him back, aren't you?"

"Harry!" I picked him up and hugged him.

Julia was staring at the bedspread. "He

likes me," she said in this really quiet voice.
"I was hoping I could keep him."

Harry was making a noise like a helicopter
warming up. He was sound asleep.

I looked over at Julia. Now that I felt sure I
was going to get home again I must have been
feeling generous. "You could always come
and visit him," I said.

HARRY'S HOMECOMING

I bet when Columbus got back home his
mother wasn't standing at the door with her
arms folded across her chest and this "I want
to have a few words with you" expression on
her face. I bet Mrs Columbus was jumping
up and down with joy. I bet she ran out to
greet him. "Chris!" she cried. "My boy's
back!" I bet she didn't ask him if he'd
brought her any souvenirs.

The first thing my mother said when we
walked through the door was, "Where's the
shopping?"

"The what?" I said.

My mother put on her overly patient

mother's voice. It's always a bad sign.

"The shopping," she said. "You know, Sara Jane, the milk and the bread and the tomatoes you were supposed to buy while you were out?"

Harry sneezed.

"Oh, Mum," I said. I couldn't slap my forehead because my arms were full of cat, but I looked pained. "I forgot all about it."

"Really?" said my mother. "What a surprise." My mother can be very sarcastic sometimes.

"It's just that, you know, it was raining so hard." I opened my anorak. "And Harry got soaked, Mum. I think he's caught a chill."

Harry sneezed again.

"I'm going to have to put him to bed," I said. I started for the hall. "He may even have a temperature."

"Not so fast," said my mother. "I think you have a little explaining to do."

I turned to face her. I was smiling. It confuses them when you smile. "Do you?"

My mother was not smiling. "Yes," said my mother, "I do. I had a very interesting phone call just before you came in."

"That's nice," I said.

"From a Mr Alvarez."

"Mr Alvarez?"

"Yes, Mr Alvarez. He seemed to know you quite well." She stared at the grey head sticking out of my jacket. "And Harry."

"Oh, that Mr Alvarez!" I was still smiling. "Yeah, he lives in the back."

"So I gather," said my mother. "He telephoned to tell you that he's sorry he called you a hooligan and that all is forgiven." Her eyes got very tiny. They were focussed on Harry. "Even the roast beef and the mess in the kitchen. He wanted to thank you for introducing him to the Andreas family."

"Thank me? Isn't that nice." I started for the stairs.

"Sara Jane!" When my mother uses that tone of voice she could stop a herd of charging rhinos, clean or otherwise.

"Mum, really," I said. "I've got a sick cat here." Harry sneezed three times in a row. "I've got to get him to bed."

"And somebody called Julia rang," said my mother.

"Julia?" That was terrific, Julia ringing already.

"Yes, she just wanted to make sure you got back all right." My mother was watching me closely. "She left her number if you want to ring her."

"That's great."

"She sounded very nice," said my mother.

"Yeah," I said. "She is."

"Does she go to your school?"

"Yeah," I said. "She does. She's new in the neighbourhood."

"Oh," said my mother, "so you've got a new friend?"

I hadn't quite thought of it like that.
"Yes, I suppose I have." Harry snuffled.
I stopped at the head of the stairs. "Mum," I said.

"Yes, Sara?"

"Do you think I could have something for Harry to eat?"

"Eat?" said my mother. "He's not too ill to eat?"

"Oh, no, I don't think so," I said. "What's that old saying? Feed a cold and starve a fever?"

"Um," said my mother. "Something like that."